Nüima Smith

Gold Stories of '49

Nüima Smith

Gold Stories of '49

ISBN/EAN: 9783743383425

Manufactured in Europe, USA, Canada, Australia, Japa

Cover: Foto ©Andreas Hilbeck / pixelio.de

Manufactured and distributed by brebook publishing software
(www.brebook.com)

Nüima Smith

Gold Stories of '49

GOLD STORIES OF '49

BY

A CALIFORNIAN

SICVT LILIVM

INTER SPINAS

BOSTON
COPELAND AND DAY
MDCCCXCVI

TO MY FATHER

THE TALES OF FORTY-NINE TOLD BY THY VOICE
WERE AS PURE GOLD. TAKE THEM AGAIN FROM ME!
CANST THOU NOT KNOW ACROSS THE DEEPS OF DEATH
HOW EVERY LINE IS INTER-WRIT WITH THEE?

SING, *Muse, the conquering of the mighty
    West,
        The peaceful battles of the timeless god!*
*Sing, Muse, the men who vanquished valiant wilds,
The old Gold Finder's glory, and their fame, —
The heroes of the march Across the Plains,
Whose dauntless souls and sinews shared the strong
Exultant passion of the Pioneers.*

*Now the Great Desert blossoms as the rose,
Corn tassels wave o'er broad Nebraska's plains.
Now gripped by steel the passive land lies prone,
Bound fast in fetters forged in liquid fire.
Splendid the making of those bands of steel
Where men like gods of old pour molten fire
Down the black night in streams of glowing white
That writhe and pulsate in the throbbing rage
Of glorious life and strength they are to bear.
Slowly as from the ponderous loom of Time
The quivering bars are shuttled into form,
And mighty engines shape them into rails;*

I   I

The flowing fire becomes a path for men,
It holds in thrall a vast wild continent.
Its seven-chained harness links the shores of sun
Fast to the snowy shores our fathers gained,
And built their forts of faith whose banners wave
From ocean unto ocean, from the bay
Where Liberty erect salutes the world
Unto the white lights of the Farallones
That flash response and beacon the far East
Beyond the Golden Gate that guards the Land of
  · Gold!

Gold Stories of Forty-Nine.

ॐ

I

THE FINDING OF THE GOLD

NOW gloriously the sudden signal came!
A gleam of gold within a hand surprised,
And lo! the vast Sierras lured the world.
The sweet Sierras!—there beside the stream
Where mountain snows flood down the rose-
filled vale,
And sunrise trembles on the little hills
That stand before the kingly white-crowned
heights,
Where sunset flames above the forest hoar,
And passion-flowers hang clustering 'neath the
figs,
And oleanders sway in rich perfume,
And orioles call matins to their mates,

3

And clouds of peach and almond blossoms droop
Above the scars of long-deserted mines, —
In bright Coloma, El Dorado's pride,
James Marshall found the gold a winter's morn,
A balmy winter's morn in Forty-Eight.

We were Coloma children, and the Man
Who found the Gold used oftentimes to come
Up to the parsonage where our roses bloomed
From Christmas unto Christmas. Always there
Were roses for a funeral or a bride
Even in winter, and in April's prime
A riot of blossoms, crimson, gold and white,
Creamy with sunshine, flushed like mountain
    dawn,
Or redder than the poppies on the hills.

'T was many years after the Gold was found,
Gone were the miners from Coloma's vale,
The heart of El Dorado wonderland,
And all was peaceful in the little town
As in an old world village. Like a dream
It seemed, that our rose-filled and quiet vale
Had once been quick with eager crowding life.
The Story of the Gold was the first tale
We used to choose when the great winter rains

Were falling fast upon our drooping flowers,
And we were grouped indoors about the hearth
Where pine cones, huge as we might compass
    round
With circling arms, like roses sprung in fire.
The quivering petals trembled to the blaze,
And reminiscent still of crackling boughs,
Distilled such odors from their hidden hearts,
Spicy and nut-sweet, fruitful of the scents
Of virgin-bodied trees, that the plain room
Seemed like a palace fragrant for the use
Of minstrels chanting of the lore of eld.

There the Gold Finder used to tell his tales,
Or oft he listened while my father told
The stories of his life in Forty-Nine,
While on the cottage hearth the pine cones blazed,
And winter made the passion-flowers forget
To cover all the trellis with the cross
That grew beside that holy wondrous bloom,
The Espiritu Santo, dove of white-winged peace,
Beneath the fig-tree, by our vine-hung door.
Beside the old Gold Finder sat his friends.
For them alone, sweet souls of sympathy,
And for their children was his tongue unloosed.
For them he told his story of that day

5

The world had news of speedily, the hour
He saw and touched the gold and found the dream,
The old-world dream of El Dorado, true!
From the first moment Marshall knew indeed
He held the key upon his hardy palm
That should unlock the West unto mankind.
A fever burned within his veins for days
From sudden joy of knowing that the race
Must know of him who held the treasure fast.
His soul cried I! and stood up strong and glad
And felt its oneness with the gods who gave.
Alone he lived through all his later days,
In his hill vineyard, guarding well the wines
His wine-press crushed from the rich mountain
    grapes;
Their cellar was a cave that burrowed far
By his hands' strength into his hillside deeps,
Concealed these pomps of his poor outward state.
His was the fortune, known of gods and men,
Always to seek and evermore to hope.
Others found riches in the mines where he
Found disappointment, and the Golden State
Gave him but four years' pension in reward
For the Discovery whose fame is one
With her fair fame.   'T is thus republics are!
With nectar of wild hopes he fed his soul,

Nor ever ceased to quaff until he died
Of the fine flavor of a coming bliss.
Behold him facing life's tremendous loss
Beside a friendly fireside telling tales! —
Maker of empires, toiler for a crust,
Hater of men, and desperate of God,
Lover of little children and the sun!

It was when the century was twelve years old,
Marshall was born upon a morn in May.
His birthplace was an Eastern town named Hope.
To him and to his people the great sea
That laves New Jersey's beaches beautiful
Was the one ocean of Columbia.

Not yet the far Pacific had become
More than a fabled water to their ken.
They lived and loved and worked, these good
    folk all,
Within a day's ride of historic ground
Where Washington had crossed the Delaware.
The stories of their fireside were of him,
And of his glorious deeds and victories.

When he had come to man's estate, the youth
Followed his country's star unto the West.

7

Three States were home to him within ten years,—
To Indiana, thence to Illinois,
And thence to the frontier where flows the
    Platte,
Moving towards sunset aye, he followed fate.

Then in his two-and-thirtieth year began
With five score comrades, good companions all,
The long, hard journey o'er the desert wilds
And o'er the unmapped mountains to the land
Of the broad Oregon ; thence pressing South
Through the great redwood forests of the North
He reached the Sacramento, and at last
In peace began to build a ranchman's home.

He loved his own free acres and the house
His two hands built to shelter him ; he loved
The comfort and the newness of content,
But more he loved his country ! When Fremont
At Sutter Buttes the Mexic arms defied,
Quick to his aid came Marshall and the men
He rallied from the valley ranchers' homes.

When the three Castros had laid down their
    swords,
And noble Andres Pico was subdued,

When the old capital was ours, and brave
The stars and stripes waved over Monterey,
And fame was echoing the name Fremont,
Came the good soldier home to find all gone
That he had toiled for one long happy year,
His cattle stolen and his roof-tree razed.
Nothing and ever nothing! He fell ill,
And while he lay in fever in a camp,
There came a Georgian woman to his aid,
Gay-hearted Jenny Wimmer. Her cool hand
Soothed the tired brow. Her smiles were heav-
   enly gifts.
She fed and nursed the soldier, and at last
The bitterness of life was touched with sweet,
And in the Wimmers' cabin once more Home
Grew real to his belief while this goodwife
Told him the story of her hardy youth.

Virginian born and Georgian reared, twice wed
Ere six-and-twenty, Jenny's wedding trips
Had been, — the first one from the Georgia hills
Out to the Iron Mountains, there — she wept —
Her first love died, then to the unknown West
The next year journeying with her Pioneer
Who blazed a trail o'er the Sierras' heights
For following thousands seven years later on.

She dreamed not of the part was still for her
When she nursed Marshall back to hope and life.
The autumn came, and Jenny's husband went
To work for Marshall, building Sutter's Mill.
Gay-hearted Jenny singing followed camp, —
The first white woman to Coloma came!
The New Year dawned, and Jenny, wont to say
The river's sands were golden, begged the men
To try and know, — these mountains might bear
    gold,
For were they not like her dear Georgia hills
Where the gold-hunters found some small reward?
Where she had been prospecting many a time,
As Jersey girls go berrying, and found
Her little pan of pay dirt more than once!
And so one morning when an Indian
Who helped the Mormon mill-hands, turned the
    sluice
At sunset, and all night the stream's swift flood
Had washed the sand and gravel from the bank,
A shining nugget sparkled on the ground
Upon a large flat stone beside the race,
And Marshall stooped and picked the nugget up.
No doubt had Jenny that it was pure gold
When to her hand and glance the bright bit came.
Her woman's heart, content with prophecy,

10

Declared she knew at sight this chosen spot!
In her soap-kettle filled with boiling lye
She plunged the nugget, where it lay all day,
But came out shining from its fiery bath.
So Jenny cried in triumph, "'T is pure gold!"
And Marshall, when at Sutter's Fort he learned,
By the new tests there made and certified,
Beyond all doubt 't was precious ore, returned
And gave the nugget to his friend's goodwife,
And Jenny always kept it, proud and glad.

When the Discovery of Gold was known,
From the American River to the Bay
Of San Francisco the excitement leaped
To fever heat, and the Sierras were
Peopled with Californians, finding gold
Beside the placers of a score of streams, —
And in a thousand gulches finding gold.
Swift flew the news to all the world, and soon
To the Sierras came a countless throng.
Marshall worked on until the mill was built,
Fulfilled his contract loyally and well,
Then took his pick and pan and joined the rest.

He saw the coming of the Argonauts!
By far Magellan came New England's sons,

Manhattan's men and Pennsylvania's pride,
And Southrons, brothers in one fervent aim,
Fearless though storms beset them as they sailed,
For ever El Dorado beckoned them,
While past the Incas' shores their ensigns flew,
And past the leagues of Montezuma's land.

The Isthmus knew the tramp of myriad feet,
And scholars saw the prophecy of song
Revealed upon the peaks of Darien.
The palm-hung river bore strange crafts, a fleet
Of boats hewed from great trees so large each one
Could bear the burdens of a score of men.
Women and children sickened sore and died,
Husbands and fathers wept — and hastened on.
From Spain to Norway passed the startling word.
From England's ports and from the shores of
    France,
From Germany and Denmark and the North
Sailed eager ships unto the new found world.
The sign went forth and Asia's silent hordes
Came to their ceaseless, noiseless, ant-like tasks.
And up and down in broad Columbia,
To all her hamlets, villages, and towns,
Her cities and her forests, pierced the sting,
The stimulus and stir of a new life.

More than all dreams that avarice could share,
More than ambition knows or words could tell,
Thrilled in the veins of men in those old days.
All that the race has felt of conquering blood,
Of love of hearthstones wherefore Death is faced,
Of fine adventure and upspringing pride,
Of glory, that new born in patriot hearts
Moves a great army to unventured war,
Fired youth with fever that resistless burned,
Made old men young, in ardor for the young
Unwooed, unknown, virgin and beckoning
   West, —
Then, rank on rank, behold the Pioneers!

II

CROSSING THE PLAINS

"TWO thousand miles from our Coloma
home,"
Began my father's stories by the fire.
The old Gold Finder listened too, and oft,
If children begged him, made the grizzlies seem
Most near and dread, by growling fierce and low;
Or shook his pipe as 't were a tomahawk,
And threatened small blond heads that nestled
close
Beside the mother sitting by the hearth,
Or from the father's breast defiance smiled.
These were the tales of many a rainy eve,
And oft repeated in the summer, when
The moonlight made the valley bright as day,
Told by the Pastor, once a Pioneer:
" Two thousand miles from the Sierra snows,
Even in the heart of the great continent,
A little town was springing into life
Beside the waters of a tideless sea.

It was Fort Dearborn still to country folk,
Not yet grown used to speak its newer name.
On all the prairies near Chicago then,
The air was filled with farewells, for the word
Had come of El Dorado's treasure found,
And mothers sobbed fond farewells to their sons,
And all the wives were sweethearts in those days,
Fast clinging to their loves who kissed, — and
    went.

" One morning in the balmy month of March
That blessed the golden spring of Forty-Nine,
There was a meet like many another known.
The Story of the Gold had all men heard,
The comrades joined their leader for the ride !
I stood that sunny morning by my horse,
Waiting to mount and ride away.   The dawn
Hung o'er the prairies and the shadowy wood.
Close at my right hand the slow Calumet
Flowed slowly northward towards Lake Michigan,
While on the left below a little knoll
The Hickory's springs made crystals for the Gulf.
I stood, and saw the first rays of the sun
Shine on the parting of the ways, while all
My comrades came from near and far, and soon
It was full morn, and ours the wondrous day."

15

Simple as Nature, tender as her love,
The leader and his men, their passion fine
Unspoken, and their patriot phrase unsung,
But how their words " To see the Country "
   still
Make old eyes shine with memory and youth!

" With souls alert we passed familiar scenes.
The poplars and the hickories bowed farewell.
An early meadow-lark sang loud good-byes.
The fields we left bare-bosomed to the sun
Prayed our return. The morning filled the
   groves
When we reached slow Des Plaines, and crossed
   the stream.

" Our horses' feet made music on the road,
Our wagons were as chariots of hope.
The Morning and the Evening that first day
Created a new Earth before we slept.
Beneath the great blue sky we rose next morn
And bathed our faces in the prairie dews,
Then on past fertile fields and amber streams
And ever onward moved our happy men.
With song and jest and many a jocund plan
We rode towards sunset for that first gay week.

But soon our merriment was changed to tears,
Our smiles turned sighs, and bravest hearts were
  chilled,
For sudden sickness smote a comrade down.
He laughed at camp-fire, died before the dawn.
Our shining spades' first toil was in the earth
Of the home State to dig for him a grave.
Beside a rivulet we chose the spot,
The spring's first green spread o'er a gentle slope.
Beneath a clump of trees they laid him down,
And listened reverent while I read the Book
Whose sacred words in this first wilderness
Committed him to silence and to God.
We journeyed on and crossed the mighty flood,
Father of Waters, in full majesty,
Past wooded islands and the further shore.
Saint Joseph was the patron saint, they said,
Of Pioneers, since in Saint Joseph's town
We filled great wagons with all needful stores,
And joined at last the thousands, rank on rank,
Who moved together 'gainst the Western wilds."

For them the mystery and pain and bliss
Of knowing Nature in her sternest moods
And in her hours of yielding new delights.
And ever more the tale was simply told : —

" By bugle blast the camps together called,
Made rules for mutual safety and for guard.
Each company then chose its captain, and
On every day another wagon led
Our company's advance, then fell to rear.
One man was leader, but each man was first
In his true turn for driving at the head,
And feeling manhood's power of mastery
Fronting the unknown in our caravan.
Each man was armed with rifle, pistol, knife,
Each wagon drawn by oxen, three good pairs
At least for every load.   On either side
Walked men on foot, and others rode one day
And walked the next.   Sometimes the horses led
Behind the wagons had no riders while
The slow advance was made.   A dozen miles
On every day the average, now six,
And often twenty, sometimes no advance.
At night the circling tents made a brave guard
For all the wagons' burdens, and the watch
Kept a look-out for thieves, — or Indians.
Even as the waves mount to the drawing tide,
By the true consciousness of law was led
In fine democracy our self-ruled host,
Our bannered host of thirty thousand men,
The wagons stretching far as eye could see.

18

" And Nature all that spring of Forty-Nine
Nurtured us, Plainsmen, in strange ways and
    sweet.
Never before had trappers or old guides
Beheld such early blessing of the grass.
The rivers' vales were velvety with green,
Abundant pasture for the patient beasts,
The toiling oxen, and the hard-rid horse
With the long trail before him.   And sometimes
New springs were found, delicious waters gave
Fresh cheer unto the Plainsmen, and the skies
Day after day and week on week were bright.
Life smiled upon the feeble with new strength,
And aged men grew youthful with delight
In the wide flowing freedom of the Plains.

" On April nights when heaven's flood-gates oped,
And peal on peal the sky's artillery boomed,
And lightnings made the midnight bright as noon,
Wrapped in our skins of buffaloes
Beneath our tents we heard the storm, and joyed
With pleasure primitive in the wild night.
One May morn we were careless, lost the trail,
And all day long traversed a barren waste,
That brought us sheer against great river bluffs.
Unfordable the stream, and dark the night,

And so we waited till next morning came,
And all the next day sought for the lost trail,
But not till sunset were we safe again
With the good company that mile on mile
Made of the wagon train a stately host
Moving with measured, solemn march and slow,
The wagons' covers white like soldiers' tents,
The buglers' welcoming call a warning, too.

"Another day, one of our oxen lamed,
We hitched a cow into his place, and she
Was ready for her share of work.   We cheered
The hard-worked beast that night.   And she
    was fed
With soft spring-grasses by a woman's hand.
Few were the families in Forty-Nine
That crossed together; later many went,
But in our caravan the wives were few,
And few the children, and their gayety
Was part of all the music of those days.
How we all smiled and wiped our eyes once
    when
Beside the camp-fires sitting a chill night,
Above the prairie stillness, soft and clear
We heard a woman's voice sing 'Home, sweet
    Home!'

" We burned long rosin-grasses, missing wood,
And thanked kind Nature for their short-lived
　　flame.
New foods we tasted, good and wild and strange.
We startled plovers winging from the grass
Beside brown streams that ever clearer grew.
The antelope, bright graces of the plain,
Lured all our huntsmen, bounding fleetly by.
We jested at our gifts from Nature's hands,
Declared the whetstones, found one bright May
　　day,
Perfect of grain beside an ochre knoll,
Were left to edge our comrades' dullard wits.
We gathered nosegays of the prairie flowers,
Huge feathery blooms of pink, or sprays of red,
And sent them to each other when at night
The music of the violin and fife,
The banjo, clarionet, and tambourine
Summoned the dancers to a camp-fire ball.
'T was pleasant too whene'er our school-bred
　　men
Sought likeness in their poets for the sound
If wolves made choruses for us by night,
And pleasant too when they took turn about
Reciting poetry sometimes for hours,
Their voices sounding in a rhythmic chant.

" Homeric came the trampling to our ears
Of the great herds of buffaloes.   Like clouds
Across the morning swept their thunderous
    trains,
And, not content, we looked for mammoths too.

" Summer had come before the Red Man crossed
The trail we followed, league by slow-passed
    league,
But one June day a band of warriors came,
A hundred Sioux, all riding like the wind,
Their bows and feathers pictured 'gainst the
    sky,
As fast with lance in rest the men came on.
I raised my hands, palms upward to the sky,
Then forth in friendship, waving them for peace.
Swift they dismounted and each warrior sat
Silent in line.   Their chieftain beckoned me,
And so I went and shook his outstretched hand.
He sought a wounded enemy we hid,
An arrow-pierced Pawnee, who, half alive,
Beside the trail one of our men had found,
And nursed him in his wagon.   I signed truth,
Kneeling I bent my head, as who should say,
' The Great Spirit cares for him.' 'T was even so.
Once more the warrior shook my hand and went.

" One day we came upon a peaceful town
Where Indian girls and women welcomed us,
Walking beside their fathers, husbands, sons,
And brave in beaded costumes, flowery gay.
Their gowns of skins were smothered with the
  beads
Bright as their eyes that stared most curiously,
At these white people who by some strange gift
Had patience for so slow and toilsome march
To find a yellow metal, useless, too,
Since who could eat or drink it when 't was found?
'T is true it would make pretty beads, but then
Such things as these they might find nearer home.

" The Indian men who from that village came
To greet us were the noblest fellows all
I e'er beheld, brown, naked to the sun
As God had fashioned them, their shapely limbs
Unfettered, strong, and splendid to be seen,
Their supple bodies, graceful and erect,
Fine with free life and vigorous with health.
When I remember them, I always think
Of my first glimpse upon the trackless plains
Of the wild horses galloping in herds,
Nobler by far than any stall-fed steeds
Can ever be, finer to look upon

Than handsomest horse e'er fed and groomed by
    men.
The wild oats fed these horses of the plains.
How hardly fared the man who dared their fire
And tried by trickery to master them !
A splendid stallion caught one starry night
By traps and ropes, defied our utmost strength
And efforts for his holding. 'Let him go !'
We cried at last, and were more proud than he
To see him bound again across the night
Defiant even of his liberty !

" How long our way beside the turbid Platte!
How fine the great reunion when at last
We met again with hundreds of our train
Scarce seen for weeks, where the Saint Joseph
    road
Rejoined the old Fort Kearney trail, and where
The great South Fork was forded turn by turn.

" Deep quicksands threatened at the best of
    fords,
And fierce the treacherous dragging at the wheels
Across its wild half-mile of waters. Yet
Old Plainsmen to this day speak of the Platte
With fond affection, for the river was

Friendly to man and beast three hundred miles.
Through storms and sunshine, across fertile lands
And treeless plains beside the Namaha,
On past the Little Blue and the Lost Run,
Still the great river was a constant friend,
And when at last it must be left behind,
Forded and conquered by our caravan,
Its quicksands had a charm for memory.

"Sometimes by fruitful valleys and clear streams,
Sometimes by fields of alkali we went,
And deserts crossed.   The first hills that we saw,
High and precipitous, of oolite rock
Based upon clay and hardening upward seemed
Domes of a great cathedral filled with hope,
Where cheerful waters would refresh us and
Thirst might be quenched in fearlessness, where
     prayer
Would quick become the natural speech of man
In gratitude and praise for perils past.

"They who are prairie born, and first behold
Majestic mountains have a keener sense
For their inspiring than those mountain-bred,
To whom the lights and shadows on the heights
Are as familiar as the fall of day.

When first I saw these distant rising hills
The tears thrilled through my very nerves and
  choked
My voice while calling all the men to come
And hasten towards those heights Delectable
Whose fair deception but postponed delight.
For still receding as the men advanced
Twice twenty miles the mountains lured them on
Before the first spurs that had seemed so near
Were reached.   And there the passing host had
  left
A thousand signals of their march and quest.

"Here men, moved by the passion of the hills,
Thrilled mightily with eagerness and pride
In the new call for all their manhood's strength,
And therefore humanly in thirst of life
Desiring speech with their Beloveds far,
Had carved on bleaching bones of buffalo,
Or skulls of antelope, long messages,
Should any choose to take them to their home.
Letters were left in crevices of rock
Fine words of hope and courage scattered round!

"To all who came those signals brought good
  cheer,

Though none would go to take the letters home
'Back to the States' for those whom Love had
    left
These letters, the fond offering of hearts
Brave for new dangers, and rejoiced to be
Here at the foot of wild tremendous heights
Yet longing for a lingering touch of those
At hearthstones far. No lyre of love-swept
    strings
Might worthy sing the flowering of faith
And tenderness in these, Love's letters, doomed
To fade and mingle with the mountain's breath,
To spend their sighs in autumn's chilling blast,
While far away were wives and maids who
    yearned
In memory of kisses — and in hope !

" On went the Pioneers ! And castled rocks
And minarets of temples hewn in stone,
Bastions of fortresses immutable,
And ruins of great cities, seemed to be
The solemn nearing mountains. Barren plains
Gave place to barren hills. Sudden before
Snow-crowned stood Laramie ! Emotion fine
Moved in a thousand hearts, yet where's the
    man

Who crossed in Forty-Nine who will not say
That Laramie is not remembered best
For home-cooked food that from the Fort was
     brought?
Forsaking pilot-bread for pie was joy
Like that of shipwrecked mariners when led
From famine unto plenty! 't was indeed
Not unlike shipwreck when a wagon failed,
Was broken, or its oxen lamed, and this
More bitter felt because the prairie craft
Could not give rescue as they hailed and passed.
But trouble waited not on that first year.
The hardships of the men of Forty-Nine
Were multiplied in Fifty. Then, indeed,
Woe and disaster, death and sin and strife,
Attended on the desperate struggling hordes.

"After our distant glimpse of Laramie
How many weary days before we reached
Sweetwater River! Sweet indeed the stream,
Refreshing to us all, both man and beast,
After the soda or the sand-filled floods,
For the last thousand miles. My memory
Of the old Rockies always is mixed in
With water, water! Ah, no one can guess
The joy of tired limbs and of aching throats

That feel delicious cold of mountain springs.
Once on the borders of a wide morass
High in a rocky gorge, in the wild pass,
We dug for water, and we found at first
A half-foot layer of transparent ice
Deep 'neath the swampy pass for months preserved,
And now revealed for our contentment while
Fiercely the sun beat on those treeless heights.
Never were ices half so eagerly
Passed on from hand to hand as buckets were
Filled with this mountain's gift to Pioneers.

" Crossing the Rockies, daily wonders grew
Strangely familiar ; huge enormous cones
Standing in isolated majesty
Passed stately by, as in a storied march ;
Red earth of buttes took tones most fanciful.
High were the stars by night, and sweet the air
Of the great table-land where antelope
And buffalo were plentiful as birds.
The Rocky Mountain Indians were at war,
But we went on in peace, nor saw them once,
Past traders' huts where half-breed children played
About the lodges.   By and by the camp
Where Simonton with troops for Oregon
Rested beside Green River Ferry.   Ah,

No words can tell how good it was to see
Our country's soldiers by that snow-fed stream!
All night across a mountain desert drear
Our weary teams and men had hardly toiled,
Not daring start beneath the July sun
Across the arid waste whose ashen soil
Cast up its suffocating clouds like waves
Of a mysterious, bitter Lake of Death.
All the dark night and all the awful day
For three-score miles, with anguish like despair
We struggled painfully, — the desert crossed,
And lay down for the night in a ravine
Too much worn out to give our cattle care
Or find the food within our wagons stored.
And then next morning in the early light
Remembering our patient, faithful beasts,
And driving them to find some water near,
Mounting a little hill we saw that camp, —
There floated dear Old Glory in the breeze!

" It was indeed a glorious Fourth for us,
That Independence Day of Forty-Nine!
Green River Ferry was a stamping-ground
Inspiring eloquence in dullest men ;
The river there flowed down through willows
    green,

And cotton-woods were growing on the banks.
Its icy waters, rushing cold and pure
From the Wind River, swept down towards the
    Gulf
That Cortes found, where Colorado's stream
Mingles its flood with those far distant seas.

" Far to the north, white-browed, magnificent,
Height upon height stupendous mountains ranged.
There, in this mighty forum of the West,
When sunset's banners floated red across
The blue of heaven and the eternal snows,
From every Plainsman's tent and from the
    camp
Where bivouacked the troops for Oregon,
Came forth the men refreshed, and cheered the
    Day.

" And when one virile voice, sonorous, clear,
Struck up the Nation's hymn, a thousand more
Joined in the grand refrain, and splendidly
Rolled forth upon the fine exalted air
The patriot chorus of the Pioneers,
Saluting there our Country and her sons.
' Land of the noble free ! '   The echoes wild
Bore on the melody to templed hills,

To every rock and rill and mountain-side
The cry exultant rose, — 'Let Freedom ring!'

" And late that eve after the tale was told
How Marcus Whitman, long before Fremont,
With his young wife had crossed these wilds to
  plant
In Oregon the standard of the faith,
And how on coming to the famous spring
In the South Pass whose waters flow both ways,
They all knelt down, while waved the stars and
  stripes,
And with their Bibles in their hands, gave thanks
For the fair unknown land they claimed for
  God, —
Again a chorus rose!   And now the stars
Shone on our men while we remembered him,
Hero and martyr, faithful priest of God
And of his country, who here too had passed.
Then soldiers joined with Plainsmen, thinking
  all
Of voices heard on Sunday morns at home ;
And mingling thoughts of love with worship's
  words,
We hymned our Maker's praises.   And the night
Received our voices, thrilled with fervor deep,

While men of many creeds with one accord
Singing aspired to crown Him Lord of all !

" Beyond Green River but a little way
We reached a grove of lovely conifers,
A wooded island on the bleak plateau,
A green oasis in a treeless land.
For three-score days no groves had we beheld,
And this deep forest bore such balms for us
As none may know who ne'er have hungered
  long
For sight of good green boughs instead of shrubs
And stunted bushes of the treeless plains.

" In the Bear River valley first we saw
Four seasons round us all in one view joined ;
Above was everlasting winter, stern
Upon the peaks unconquered, and below
The summer plain, while round about us spread
The flowers of spring and fruits of autumn grew.
On past the Bear Spring geysers, and the cones
Of spent volcanoes, through romantic dales
To the Snake River country where no guard
Was needed for our camp, the natives there
Were all such Christian heathen.   But the snakes !
Enormous reptiles dared our bravest men.

3   33

The terror of Eve's daughters was our own
Although we left full many a rattler dead.
The Humboldt deserts brought our hardest days,
The dread, mysterious Basin was a foe
Unconquerable to many a traveller.
After the mountain springs a fortnight's toil
Where no grass grew, where the oases were
More rare than angels' visits, and the sun,
The August sun, shone glaring on our camp,
Where night by night we struggled sadly on.
In the long caravan there sickened then
All of the feeble, and death daily came
Through one long week, and claimed a sufferer.
None of my friends, 't is true, were called to
    mourn,
But all are friends in such sore straits.   Aye, oft
When tired and worn and ready to despair
I have seen men give one another care,
Forgetful of their own keen sufferings,
Holding the can of precious water close
To parching lips, smiling till staring eyes
Drooped into rest, and breath came softly back.

"The Indians here were troublesome, and guard
Was constant and at times there came
From trains ahead the news of plundering.

On through gaunt sage-brush, torment of the
    plains,
Our trail was past the salt springs, and the hot,
And death in life seemed every burning day.

"There came at last a brilliant August eve,
After the last oasis had been passed,
When the great mountains that had grown more
    near
In dim high splendors, flung their crests of snow
Against the glories of a violet sky.

The great Sierras in the sunset stood,
And soon each rugged peak that towered white
Above its rolling snowy fields grew red.
Shining Sierras, beaconing to us, burned
Like great red lamps above the Land of Gold.

" Peace like a river flowed when the first streams
Of sweet hill-water we at last had gained,
And hastening onward through the wild ravines
Or the black cañons of the foothills, found
Rest in the deep pine forest of a vale
High on the mountain-side, where colonnades
Of mighty trees roofed o'er our little band.
Soft fathomless shadows wrapped us in content.

We lay and rested while the rivulets
Sung melodies for us more sweet than song.
Cool, solemn, pillared, rose the noble pines,
And as we lay full length upon the ground
Up from their boles to their great waving tops
The light of heaven seemed toying with the
    shade,
Until the high boughs melted with the wind
That murmured there, and light and sound seemed
    one.
Then, tired men all, we slept until the call
Came from the camp for workers! Supper now
Was no more bacon, but the mountain trout.

" For twenty days Sierra passes through
Our happy men rode onward. Troubles were
Light as our spirits, and the day we found
The first pale slate whose outcrop pledges gold
Was such a day as makes all hardship dear!
And scarce the wiser heads could keep the
    young
From leaving all and setting forth alone
To Feather River and Grass Valley where
The diggings were the richest. But the need
Of guard against the Indians kept the men
Still in large bands; the need indeed was great.

36

" And now prospecting kept us all alert
For golden findings, but our pans were used
More to boil coffee than to wash out gold
Until we all had reached the trading camp,
Over the mountains.   Welcome was the sight
Of habitations that at least were homes
In that they moved not on from day to day.
How our hearts bounded when upon the heights
We first beheld the camp!   Like men at sea
Tossed by the waters to a longed-for shore
We reached the adobe houses and the tents,
And heard of the new city that had sprung
Into full life while we were on the way!
To Sacramento many went at first
To get provisions and prepare anew,
While we impatient ones made haste to come
To El Dorado and her famous mines.

" Here men made fortunes, here were fortunes lost
In placers and in quartz.   Here gaming grew
To be a fiercer fever than the fire
Which burned in men for riches, but withal
There was a wild nobility of soul
Ruled lawless men in those old golden days.
From camp to loyal camp there stretched a bond
That knitted men together in the strife'

And made each outlaw and each gentleman
One in the pride to hurt no helpless one,
That scorned all falsity and branded black
All lack of brother's faith as worse than sin.
A man was sure to find good friends if he
Was friendly unto men, and this when he
Panned out a thousand dollars or but one."

" And, father, did you find great heaps of gold?"
A childish voice would ask. The Pastor smiled, —
" I found a little now and then, not much,
But just enough to take me back next year
In swift ships by the Isthmus to the States,
And, by and by, bring here with me again
One who is worth her weight in gold, you know."
And here his brown eyes at the blue eyes smiled
That ever smiled again at him, and us, —
One who loved well Coloma.   And the vale
Where the white roses bloom forgets her not.
Ah, dear Coloma!   There these tales were told
A thousand times more picturesque and strong
Than here set down, with countless details more,
But always ending, while the Pastor smiled,
As the old stories end, — " And so they all
Lived happy ever after and in peace."

III

THE LOST GOLD LAKE

THERE was another tale more strange
than all
Told one June eve beneath the spread-
ing fig.
The river's ripples murmured from the sands,
And turtle-doves cooed in the tender dusk
Where lilies breathed and ruddy poppies drowsed.
The mocking birds called from the wood.   The
air
Was soft with breath of roses.   All the vale
Slumbered in fragrance, but the chaparral
And manzanita on the mountain-side
Stirred, as by wandering spirits gently touched.
Above the cedars hung a tawny moon,
And the sweet starry sky seemed strangely near.

The old Gold Finder had been sitting long
In silence.   He had seen himself revealed,
His simple, stern, heroic figure strong

In the clear foreground of the Early Days,
When he was herald to the Pioneers.

At last he spoke as by some sacred law
Forced to complete the story and declare
Why in these latter days men saw him oft,
A white-haired mystic, wandering on the hills
Of El Dorado, seeking aye to find
What ne'er again he was ordained to find.
Perchance his secret still is for the world,
For still the snow Sierras guard its key,
And still the Golden Lake remains unfound.

Through all his months and years he sought to find
Once more the way unto the Lost Gold Lake.
There came a day he died when far from home,
And men incredulous of him, their Seer,
Brought back his brave and undefeated clay,
And buried him where first he found the gold
In bright Coloma, on his vine-clad hill.

There California hath honored him.
His monument is beacon to the vale
Above the brook whose murmuring waters fall
Into the mountain river's singing deeps —
Cold with the snows — that chant his requiem.

It was in the high Sierras, thus the tale,
That the Discoverer found the Golden Lake.
He had been gone from home for many a day.
Huge live-oaks sheltered him, and wild fruits gave
Of their abundance.   Evermore he sought
For signs of precious metal.   Evermore
Pure goldless crystals urged him on and on,
Still seeking for the slate whose pallid hue
Is roseate unto a hope deferred,
In strange deep cañons never found before,
Where clustering redwoods shut the sunlight out,
And mosses tapestried black cavern doors
Along the mountain-side with brilliant grey
Shot through with woof of rose and amethyst.

It was the evening of a weary day,
He stood surrounded by bright mica knolls,
That mocked him with their glitter.   All about
They shimmered with false splendors.   Sunset fell.
Full forty yellow summits faded dun
Above a plain, vast, bleak, and desolate.

Sudden he saw, deep in a dark ravine
That pierced a path between two sombre heights,
A shining doorway, softly radiant.
Swiftly he neared the portal, pausing there,

For murmurs came of faint enchantments, — faint
As songs in dreamland heard, an anthem borne
Upon the winds from echoes lulled to sleep
Within earth's bosom.   When the music ceased
He entered in, while paled the radiance
Upon the columns of this temple chaste
And worshipful, hewed from the mountain's heart.

Long plumes of fretted stone hung motionless
From the great vault, or waving seemed to cling
To lofty pillars set in solemn rows
Of lustrous alabaster, milky white,
And marshalling between them in the dusk
Upspringing stalagmites so crystal fine
That every facet shone like Pleiad pure,
And exquisite with myriad tints of pearl.

Far in the holy cavern was a shrine
Where the clear waters of a little spring
Dripped from the shadows down into a font
Below a cross worn in the living stone
By the baptismal waters.   There he knelt
Praying for freedom from his torturing dream
Of golden wonders still for him to find.
Even as he prayed he slumbered, sinking down
Beside the altar and the crystal font.

And as he wakened with the new-born light,
Lo! mystic whispers came: *On the third day!*
On the third day! On the third day! he heard,
Repeated thrice.   He rushed forth from the cave,
And turned not back to his fair refuge more,
Nor glanced again at its serene retreat.
Onward he fared! Morning had come and hope.

All day he wandered through grim cañons, and
Through all the starless night paused not, nor
  slept.
He heard the moaning of the forest beasts
In troubled slumbers, and the faint far cry
Of midnight masters of the upper world
Where music melts from every icy rill.
And all the second day, and all the night
He followed the strange whispers whose portent
Promised him more than mortal breath might
  speak.

On the third morrow, ere the silver dawn
Had touched the sleeping valleys, ere the East
Had shown the stars a first soft plighting ray,
At that deep hour when all the wild things wake,
When windless nights stir suddenly with life,
And men who stand bare-browed unto the sky

Learn infinite secrets of the universe, —
He paused before a monument of snow,
The first white dome above the growing world.
The last king pines knelt captive at his feet,
Obeisance murmuring, and the morning star,
Mellowing the darkness, gleamed upon the way
That led up steep pure heights. And, as he stood,
Across the snow shone forth a crimson glow.
Now here, now yon, it flashed in flowers of flame
Like those of little cones upon the hearth
In valley homes when winter fires are low.

Onward he pressed.   The morning star grew
    pale,
While gliding o'er the peaks dawn silvery came.
A second snowy dome loomed vast before,
And on its right another.   These twin guards,
Dividing like a gate the broad white way,
Narrowed his path ; and as he stood between
Before him lay the Garden of the Snows !

Small crimson flowers flamed at his feet.   They
    grew
Waving their tiny petals in the air
Far, far above the last forgotten pines.
His mind refused its credence to his eyes,

44

And doubt bedewed his lashes with a mist.
A sweet keen languor pierced his very veins,
And slow he sank upon the earth's white breast.

Then while he lay and watched the crimson
  flowers
Majestic glories flashed across the North,
Dimming the East and filling heaven with fire.
The spacious vault was luminous, the morn
Suffused with heavenly ardors. Streamers swelled
And arched as by celestial breezes swayed.
Lustrous were all the near and utmost peaks
Of ranged Sierras, yearning upward, faint
With passion of reflection. Banners gold,
Crimson and violet, undulated slow,
Blended with floating azure chains and green
In exquisite confusion, or thrilled white,
Or deepened to that tint of marvel pale
Named amber of Chaldean seers, who
Beheld their mountains and its color one!

Even as he gazed the Night's Aurora fled
To the embrace of her pure sister Morn,
And, soul in soul, they met the conquering Sun.
He gazed and saw the crimson flowers fade pink.
Paler they grew as seashells in the dusk

While whispering ocean kisses a lone beach.
Then up he rose, as warm of spirit and sense
As if beside his hearthstone when the log
Had kept its living coals all day and night.
Erect he stood.   Beyond the hither gates
Of the fair vanished Garden of the Snows,
He saw again two domes immense and pure,
So icy pure the sun's expanding rays
Bathed the great crystals in irradiate floods
Of light less luminous than theirs.   Once more
He heard the whispers whose portents obeyed
Bring wonders manifold to mortal ken.
They bade him Follow !   As his footsteps crossed
The Garden of the Snows, where'er he trod
Fresh blossoms started into fragrant life.
Before the twin White Gates he paused.
Nor fear, nor chilling horror grasped his soul,
But fierce he felt the joy of the Unknown
And palpitated with the bliss of Death :
Enchanted by its mystery, he passed
The portals swift, — and came unto his dream !
An azure summer Lake embosomed there
Mirrored the high blue skÿ.   Lapping its shore
Were little waves that broke against the strand
In harmonies like an Æolian harp

When breath of happy prayers has swept the
  strings
Of a nun's casement as she gives her youth, —
Ah, mystic bride! — and leans to Heaven by
  night.

Across the Golden Lake sweet zephyrs strayed
Bringing rare balsams, Alpine fragrances,
Subtler than those that flow from Shasta's mount,
Odors undreamed on Tahoe's lovely shores, —
Soft moonbeam scents like breath of fairy isles.
He heard wild music of an unseen bird
That poured its soul in jubilance of song
And trilled and called and carolled loud and
  clear
As his heart's music beating joyously.
Along the shining sands he slowly walked,
And knew before he held them in his hands,
Here was his treasure, found at last unsought.
He lay beside the waters, breast to earth.
He stripped, and in their warmth his limbs he
  laved,
And pressed his body to their sands of gold,
While o'er him swept the little billowing waves
In the first shallows of that hidden sea.

Upon the Lake he floated silently,
Or turned and with swift strokes the bright depths
  cleaved,
And saw the endless shimmer of fine gold
Below the paths of rainbow fish that played
Among the mosses fringing the far shore.
Against the bank a strangely tufted hedge
Concealed what lay beyond : content he sped
Lusty with manhood to the hither shore.
He made a bower of interlacing boughs
From a dark tree like cedars of the vale,
And in the purple shade lay down to rest.
But Joy had taken his hand and would not bide.
She pressed him with wild clamors at his breast,
She smiled and clasped him, and fled down the
  shore.
She blessed his soul, and warmed his body through
With rapturous intent as fast he ran
Beneath the brilliant skies, and fast returned,
While close beside him, sweet and eagerly
He felt her fleeting, — and the bliss of breath !
Loud sang the unseen bird, and drew more
  near
Flitting across the voiceless space of air,
And hiding in the shadow of the bower.

48

He knelt beside the bower, and spread his palms
Unto the bending heavens, — then aloud
Shouting and singing, frenzied with delight
Roused a great chorus into glorious song.
From each empurpled shade, each bush and shrub,
From wild-flower trees, in feathery snow of bloom,
And from the skies and the encircling hills
Came riotous ecstasy of rich response.
Gladder than nightingales that sing by day
In Eastern gardens, louder than the lark
Of prairie meadows, sweet as orioles
That herald sunrise to their sleeping loves,
In melody rejoiced the unseen choir.

Close by the bower wild luscious fruits he found,
Tropic with sweet, red as pomegranates are
That grow in Cascade valleys, next the sea,
But missing all the tantalizing lure
Of those strange apples; these made hunger kind,
Blessed him in eating, and refreshed his sense,
And added to his very soul's content.

Along the shore, the converse way he strolled
And here found pebbles strewn upon the beach
By playful waves, great nuggets of pure ore!

4   49

As children build a house, so one by one
He piled about him the bright glittering stones,
And row on row and line on line upreared
A golden cabin, toiling all day long.
He roofed it with the unknown cedar's boughs,
Then once more of the strange pomegranates ate,
And lay him down to rest, while evening came.
An hour half waking, half in sleep's embrace
He dreamed a future marvellous and kind.
Empires of grandeur passed before his mind,
Swift argosies saluted him, with sails
Set for a thousand happy ports, and kings
Envied his El Dorado, first of earth.
He built a thousand homes in heart's delight,
And every orphaned child with mothering care
Was nurtured, rocked at night, and kissed to sleep,
And given May Day roses every morn.

Lo! as he dreamed, ere yet he had desired
To use his lore of wood-craft and the skies,
To know which way to guide his thronging camp
Even as he dreamed, a hurricane came down.
A great wind reared the waters of the Lake
That dashed in mad black breakers at his feet,
Whelming his wonder world in wrathful night.

A nameless terror seized him, and he fled,
Wrapping his garments to his trembling frame.
He passed the great White Gates, turned tempest
 dark,
And onward through the Garden of the Snows,
Whose blood-red blossoms withered impotent
And seedless fell about his flying steps.
Two nights and days all through the dreadful
 storm
Homeward he hastened, led of unseen guides
Down great volcanic gorges rent and torn
From out the mountain fires and shuddering still
With flames in wide black craters cold and spent.
On either side of him strange mountains raised
High glittering crests, and pale cliffs towering dim
Crumbled and fell on either side his way.

'T was on the third dark evening, ere the storm
Had died within the valley, once again
Beside his hearth he sat, and tasted bread.
His hair and beard dead white about him hung,
And in his eyes a strange light deepening burned,
Quenched not thereafter.   In his palm he bore,
Clasped fast in his first agony of fear,
Three gleaming golden grains, — his harvest proof!

And thus the story ended.   So Good Night,
The old Gold Finder said, and went his way.
The moon shone royally above the hill,
Lighting the path up to his lonely home.

THIS BOOK IS PRINTED BY
JOHN WILSON AND SON DURING
OCTOBER 1896